Michael Whaite

100 DOGS

PUFFIN

Small dog,

tall dog,

playing with a **ball** dog,

big dog,

dig dog, burying a bone . . .

Old dog, cold dog, doing as he's told dog,

bad dog, sad dog, sitting all alone.

Shaggy
dog,

baggy
dog,

Wag-Wag-Waggy
dog,

Woofy
dog,

fluffy
dog,

always looking
scruffy
dog,

dirty dog, squirty dog,
watering
a tree.

bossed
dog,

LOST DOG!

Where can
he be?

HAPPY DOG

snappy dog,

yap yap yappy dog,

proud dog,

loud dog,

scratching at the door.

Pug dog, snug dog,

chewing on the rug dog,

Song dog, strong dog, that's a very **l o n g** dog,

Tiny dog, whiny dog, shampoo shiny dog,

whiffy dog, **sniffy** dog,

searching for clues . . .

cool dog, **drool** dog,

ruining your shoes **!**

frizzy dog,

whizzy dog,

spin around **dizzy** dog,

drag dog,

bag dog,
carried everywhere!

Stay dog, Play dog,

red dog,

here to
save the day
dog,

sled dog,

dashing through
the snow.

Leap dog,

sheep dog,

MOP dog,

fallen fast **asleep** dog,

top dog,

BEST IN SHOW!

Achy dog, flaky dog, shivery and shaky dog,

twitchy dog, itchy dog, covered in fleas.

Pull dog, bull dog,

feeling very full dog,

hot dog, squat dog –

pick it up please!

Chase dog,

race dog,

Star dog,

car dog,

that looks so **bizarre** dog,

loyal dog, royal dog,

living like a king!

Guide dog, dyed dog,

Scottie dog, spotty dog, sniffing at a botty dog,

very, very **wide** dog,

chew dog,

new dog –

so cute!
Awww . . .

yellow dog,

hello dog,

shaking a paw.

WONDER DOG

under dog,

Cute dog,

toot dog,

boot dog,

scoot dog,

hound dog,

found dog . . .

which dog's

PUFFIN BOOKS

UK | USA | Canada | Ireland | Australia
India | New Zealand | South Africa

Puffin Books is part of the Penguin Random House group of companies
whose addresses can be found at global.penguinrandomhouse.com.

www.penguin.co.uk   www.puffin.co.uk   www.ladybird.co.uk

 Penguin
Random House
UK

First published 2018
001

Copyright © Michael Whaite, 2018
The moral right of the author has been asserted

Printed in China
A CIP catalogue record for this book is available from the British Library

ISBN: 978-0-241-34781-2

All correspondence to:
Puffin Books, Penguin Random House Children's, 80 Strand, London WC2R 0RL

Did you spot Lost Dog?

for
Karl + Fran